STECK-VAUGHN BOLDPRINT® kids

Stand Tall

Edited by David Booth

Steck-Vaughn®

HOUGHTON MIFFLIN HARCOURT

10801 N. Mopac Expressway
Building # 3
Austin, TX 78759
1.800.531.5015

Steck-Vaughn is a trademark of HMH Supplemental Publishers Inc. registered in the United States of America and/or other jurisdictions. All inquiries should be mailed to HMH Supplemental Publishers Inc., P.O. Box 27010, Austin, TX 78755.

Rubicon
www.rubiconpublishing.com

Associate Publisher: Wendy Cochran
Editor: Dawna McKinnon
Creative/Art Director: Jennifer Drew
Senior Designer: Gabriela Castillo
Designer: Rebecca Buchanan
Cover image–iStockphoto.com; title page–Shutterstock.com

Jean Little: "Sticks and Stones" from *I Gave My Mom a Castle*. Permission courtesy of ORCA BOOK PUBLISHERS, Victoria, BC, Canada (2003).

Printed in Singapore

ISBN: 978-1-77058-467-9
5 6 7 8 9 10 11 12 13 14 2016 25 24 23 22 21 20 19 18 17 16
4500568939

Contents

STAND TALL!

© ISTOCKPHOTO

NAMES WILL NEVER HURT ME

Art by Luke Markle

Sticks and stones,
Stones and sticks,
Bullies use
The meanest tricks.

Never mind, my best friend says,
Those kids will go away,
What they said will disappear,
Just turn the other way.

I know that what they say to me,
Isn't really true,
But still it stings and hurts inside,
I don't know what to do.

But when my friends begin to say
The rhyme out loud and clear,
I turn around and face the world
And forget about my fear.

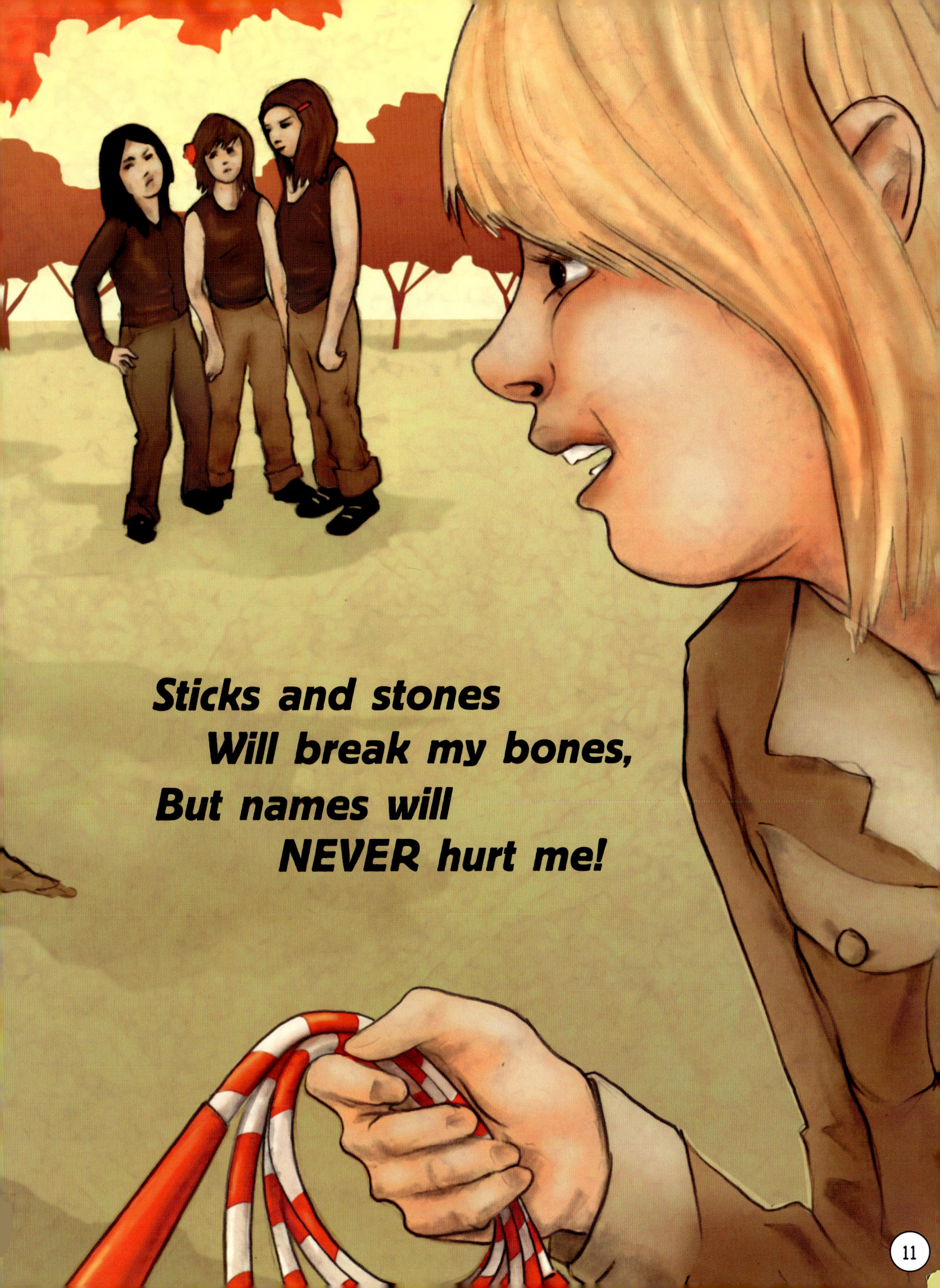

Sticks and stones
Will break my bones,
But names will
NEVER hurt me!

What Is a Bully?

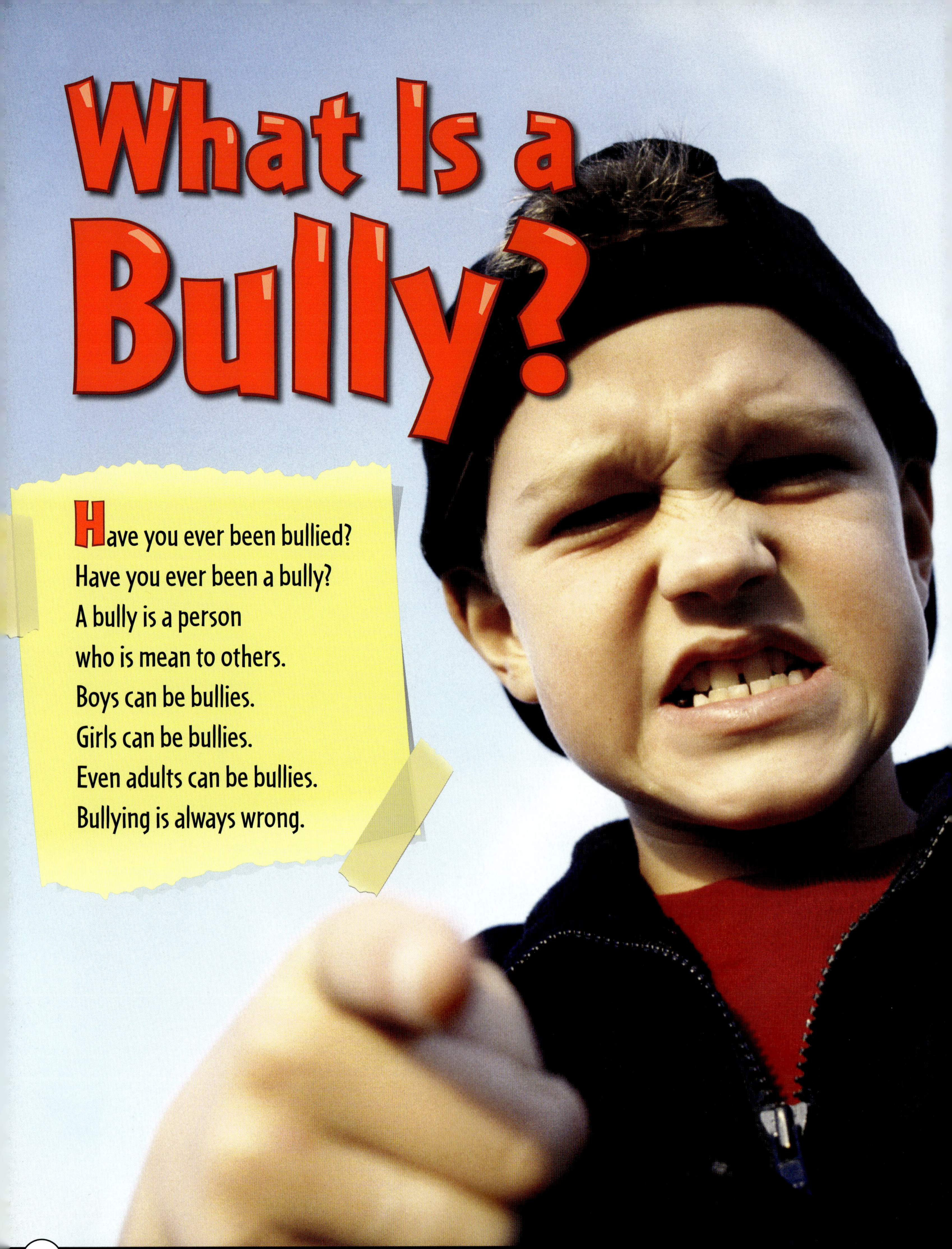

Have you ever been bullied?
Have you ever been a bully?
A bully is a person
who is mean to others.
Boys can be bullies.
Girls can be bullies.
Even adults can be bullies.
Bullying is always wrong.

There are different ways a bully can hurt someone. Here are some things a bully might do:

Call you names

Hurt you by fighting with you

Make fun of you

Talk about you behind your back

Make fun of your friends or family

Try to take something from you

Try to make you do something you don't want to

Write mean things about you online

Tell others not to be your friends

Damage your things

Where does bullying happen?

Bullies often bully people in places where others won't see them. It can happen anywhere.

It can happen:

- On the schoolyard
- Online
- At a friend's house
- On stairways
- In bathrooms
- In hallways
- At home
- In parks
- In libraries

Why do people bully?

Sometimes bullies think no one likes them, so they bully to get attention.

A bully might be jealous of others.

Sometimes bullies think they look important.

Bullies like to have power.

Some bullies are angry about something that is happening to them.

A bully might be copying something bad that happened.

A bully might just be looking for a friend.

ALL IMAGES-SHUTTERSTOCK/ ISTOCKPHOTO

Bullying can make you feel scared and all alone. Remember: a bully should never win!

Stop a Bully

There are different things you can do to make sure bullying doesn't happen to you or those around you. Check out "10 Ways to Stop a Bully" to find out what you can do.

ALL IMAGES–SHUTTERSTOCK/ ISTOCKPHOTO

STICKS AND STONES

By Jean Little • From *I Gave My Mom a Castle* • Art by Christine Tripp

When my dad was a kid,
He got picked on.
"Laugh it off," his dad told him.
"Sticks and stones may break your bones,
But names will never hurt you," his mother said.
He couldn't laugh.
The names did hurt.
Once in awhile there were sticks and stones too.

Barney Hutton and his friends began picking on me.
I wear thick glasses.
My name is Mortimer after my granddad.
And I'm small — so far,
A lot smaller than Barney.
I also wear one hearing aid.
"Shortie Mortie," he calls me.
And other names.
"Tin ear."

My dad went to the school to complain.
Miss Weller, my teacher,
Told him children were more thoughtful now.

"I've never once seen anyone pick on
Mortimer," she told him.

My dad looked at her.
Then he said, very quietly,
"Nobody picked on me either —
When the teacher was looking."

My dad is really tall.
The teacher looked up to him.
"I can talk to the principal," she said.
"But it isn't happening
on school property."

Dad went to see Barney's folks.
They said Barney wouldn't pick on anybody.
But they must have yelled at him after Dad left.
Things are slightly better.

Sticks and stones and names still hurt.
And laughing isn't such a great shield.
What I really want is somebody on my side.
What I need is a big friend.

About Jean Little

Jean Little was born in Taiwan.
She moved to Canada
when she was seven years old.
Jean was born with an eye condition.
She is legally blind.

Jean was often teased as a child,
but she stayed positive.
She did not let her condition
stop her from doing things.
Jean has written more than 25 children's books
and has won many awards.
She writes using a talking computer.

JEAN LITTLE–PHOTO COURTESY OF DAVID JOHNSTON; FLOWERS–SHUTTERSTOCK

10 Ways to STOP a Bully

It is important to stand up to bullying. Once you give in to a bully, it can be hard to stop. Keeping the problem inside won't make it go away. Challenging a bully can be difficult but you don't have to do it on your own.

Here are some different ways to stop a bully.

ALL IMAGES–ISTOCKPHOTO

1 Tell an Adult

Tell a parent, a teacher,
or someone in your community
if you are being bullied.

2 Don't Bully a Bully

Bullying is wrong.
You don't want to make someone else
feel as bad as you feel.

3 Don't Hit Back

Some people say hitting back
will stop the bullying.
If you hit a bully,
you might get hurt
or even get in trouble.
It could also make the bully
want to hurt you more.

ALL IMAGES–SHUTTERSTOCK/ ISTOCKPHOTO

4 Don't Stand By Silently

If you see someone else being bullied, it is important to help the person. Tell an adult what's going on.

5 Ignore the Bully

If a bully says something hurtful, try ignoring him or her the first time. Bullies like power and it might be enough to make them stop. If they do it again, tell someone.

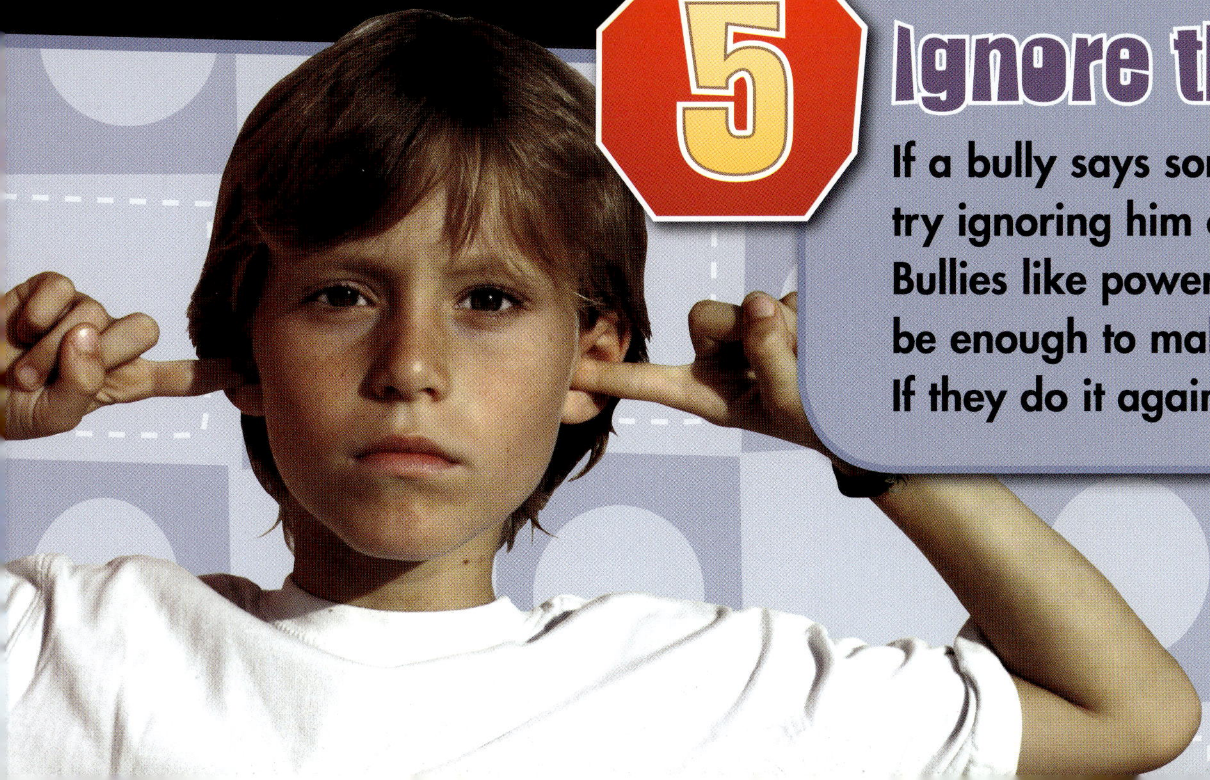

6 Say Something Nice

If a bully says something mean, pretend he or she has said something nice. You can even say, "Thank you." This can really throw off a bully!

ALL IMAGES—SHUTTERSTOCK

7 Stay in a Group

It's important to have friends who can watch out for you. Bullying doesn't usually happen to someone in a group. If you are alone, try to stay in areas where there are adults.

8 Stop a Cyber Bully

If you are being bullied online, you can block the person from contacting you. Don't open their e-mails or answer their messages.

9 Be Honest

Don't be afraid to let others know you are sad or afraid.

Practice, Practice, Practice! 10

If you know you are going to have to face a bully, practice what you will say. You can practice with friends or in front of a mirror. You will be prepared and ready when the time comes to stand tall!

I Won't Stand By

By Suzanne Muir
Art by Shingo Shimizu

We were making costumes for the school play.

They called him names that made him cry.
I just stood by.

We were playing basketball during recess.
She wanted to join in.
I just stood by.
Boys only!
They played mean tricks on smaller kids.
I just stood by.
You better not tell!
They tricked him into saying bad words because he didn't know English yet.
I just stood by.

They pretended to bump into her wheelchair by accident.
I just stood by.
Oops!
Ouch!
They took his lunch money every day.
I just stood by.
It's OK ...
his dad is rich!
They picked on her because her skin color was different from theirs.
I just stood by.
They said if I ever told on them I would be next.

Then one day they weren't my friends anymore.
You're not cool enough.
You don't wear the right clothes.
I walked the playground alone and no one talked to me.
They just stood by.

We were making costumes for the school play. They called him names that made him cry.
I held his hand.
I DIDN'T stand by.

We were playing basketball during recess. She wanted to join in.
No girls!
Come with me.
I took her to another net and let everyone play.
I DIDN'T stand by.

They played mean tricks on smaller kids.
Walk over here.
MATH
I showed those kids how to walk near the teacher.
I DIDN'T stand by.

They tricked him into saying bad words because he didn't know English yet.
Say it like this ...
I helped him to say the right words.
I DIDN'T stand by.

They pretended to bump into her wheelchair by accident.
I'll stay with you.
I walked down the hall with her.
I DIDN'T stand by.

They took his lunch money every day.
Not this time!
Together we stood up to them.
I DIDN'T stand by.

They picked on her because
her skin color was different from theirs.
I like you
the way you are!
I DIDN'T stand by.

They threatened me and they tried
to make everyone hate me ...
but it didn't work because now
I have friends who really care.

After a while they stopped bullying people and everyone feels better now because ...

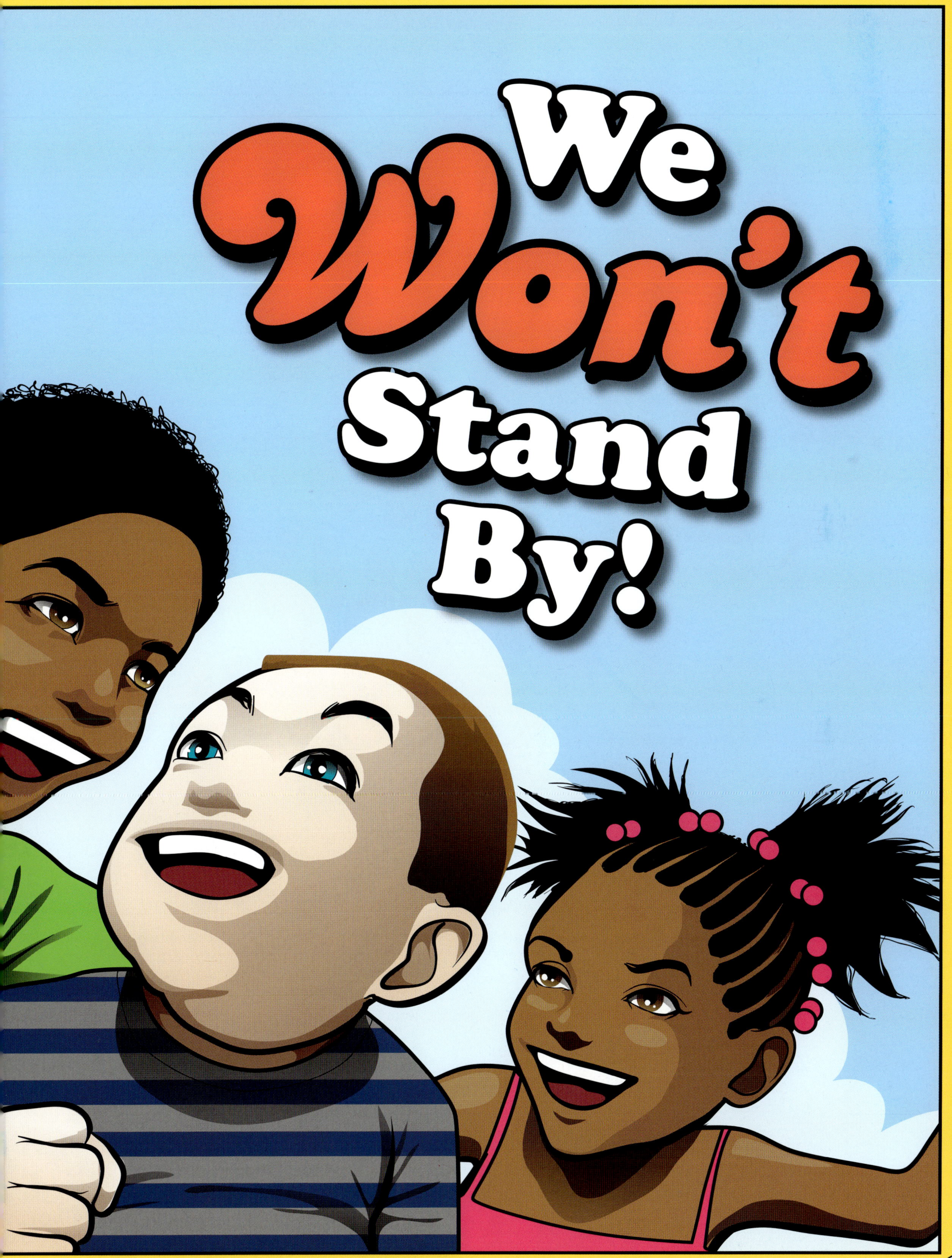
We Won't Stand By!

Bully-Free
Zone!
NO
BULLYING
ALLOWED!

Make your own poster to show that your school is a bully-free zone.

High-Frequency Words

begin	hurt	inside	mean
mind	really	still	world
behind	different	even	ever
family	fight	important	might
park	person	place	scared
someone	something	talk	try
write	began	children	couldn't
doing	eye	great	hear
laugh	move	need	often
pick	seen	seven	side
small	stay	teacher	told
wouldn't	answer	being	else
enough	face	front	group
hard	keep	nice	problem
ready	thank	throw	time
trouble	watch	care	clothes
didn't	during	everyone	lunch
money	show	stood	together
took	tried		